STEPPING INTO THEIR SHOES

.... giving them wings to fly

Novel by

Neeti Saharan

Edited by

Shweta Batra

RG
books

Published By

Redgrab Books Pvt. Ltd.

942, Mutthiganj, Prayagraj, 211003
www.redgrabbooks.com
contact@redgrabbooks.com

Price in india : 200/- INR

First published by Redgrab Books in 2022
Copyright © 2022 Redgrab Books Pvt. Ltd.
Copyright Text © 2022 Neeti Saharan
Printed and bound in India
Cover Design & Typesetting by Redgrab Books team

ISBN : 978-93-90944-55-2

INTRODUCTION

When we say adults, we can briefly divide them into the elders and the youngsters.

Apart from a vast wealth of knowledge, the elders of our society come with precious and priceless experiences.

On the other hand, our youngsters are zestful, vibrant, energetic, intelligent, innovative, and always on the go.

One cannot imagine the output when the two work in sync… it could be miraculous… but unfortunately, both seem to, for not any valid reasons, misunderstand each other. More often, the misunderstandings are apprehensions and presumptions.

This straightforward book comes to all of you like a small gift written in simple language and genuine spirit. It denotes that we all can learn from the other…age no bar.

Each chapter of this book depicts one incident that became a learning experience for the narrator.

This book intends to make the young realize that the world is a beautiful place to live…Live it to the fullest, enjoy every moment, and make an effort to make it suitable for others - A happy soul always spreads happiness.

It reminds the elders to go back to their lives, try not to label the youngsters but bring them to talk at the table and help them sort their thoughts out.

Let each one 'give' to the other in any small way and help re-built and maintain healthy, strong, cordial, and progressive relationships making the society more substantial and better.

This book might also help clear some rooted misunderstandings between the two generations and help them understand each other, build confidence to confess, and live happily ever after.

To each of us, try and be a good human and stay blissful throughout life.

PREFACE

I often observed that the adults share a very uncanny and awkward relationship, be it our elders or youngsters. Respect is a rare emotion on one end and talking ill of, making fun of, and taking them for granted is so very common on the other end. Advice/ suggestion is considered interference!

I have come across many people from all age groups. We will make fewer mistakes in life if we learn from each other's experiences, care to share our experiences with others, and learn from that. The only criteria that needed to be at peace were that one is ready to share and the other is receptive and adaptive.

Since I was already one book old, (my first book- a self-help book, 'It's time to live again' discussed, simple life problems that complicate our thought processes. Solutions given in the book were also straightforward.) I thought of writing and sharing my thoughts on bridging the gap between the two generations and bringing them together. I was not very sure how to do it but was sure I Have To Do It!

When intentions are clear, the path gets clearer …

One day, I met a friend who told me how a young girl had helped my friend find out her strengths, because of which my friend went out to become an entrepreneur!! I asked her if, like her, would people share their life-changing experiences with me, which I could further transfer to the world? My friend was very encouraging and positive and suggested that only I may need to change names respecting their privacy. I thanked her a ton.

I immediately agreed to this and started talking to more and more people, asking about their success and failure stories-some were reluctant; some said no, and the others asked me to keep their names a secret. Initially, I thought if they were not willing to share their names, their experiences might not seem authentic, which held me back for some time. But, their transforming experiences were relevant, accurate, and worthy of being shared- this thought compelled me to agree with their condition, and I began putting their words of wisdom together.

I was so happy that my dream was coming true. I used to make an appointment with the people I knew or their friends and acquaintances. I used to squeeze out time from my daily routine as writing has been my passion, and writing something so close to my heart was so exciting. We would have casual meetings, and I would jot down points as they narrated their instances to me. I realized that we just see the success of a person but not the journey of ups and downs.

During this one year, I encountered personal and professional challenges, but at no point did I drop the idea of showing this book the light of the day.

ACKNOWLEDGEMENT

The different mindsets in these beautiful minds in this beautiful life, I am thankful for how they came into my life. I enjoyed meeting each person and have always tried to adopt the best that I find in the ones I meet. Eventually, it has helped me give my best in every problematic or controversial situation I have been in!

When people haven't known me for long, they tend to think I am being pretentious but gradually gather that I am the way I am… and I am okay with it because at no point am I harmed nor ever have intentions of harming anyone.

I thank life for coming to me in its best possible way and helping me share things in the best possible ways. I have made mistakes in life and learned from them- as we say that every experience teaches you… To err is human.

To begin with, I would like to thank all those people who have, so honestly, shared their real-life instances with me. Those instances taught them a new lesson and gave their lives a new meaning. And hereon, this book may change several lives for the better. I sincerely hope I have done justice while projecting their experiences.

Special thanks with a bow to my mother, Mrs. Promila Jaitly for bringing me up in a manner where adapting to new situations was taught playfully, and I imbibed the values with love naturally- all this prepared me well to face life …find the best in each case, circumstance, or challenge to the fullest.

I acknowledge and appreciate my family and friends for believing in me and having that unshakable faith and trust in me. Gratitude to all who inspired me to write this book though I had never thought of doing such a thing earlier in life.

I am grateful to my friend Shweta Batra for being my best critic and editor of this book. This book would not have been possible without her constant support and input.

Above all, I thank my husband Shyam Saharan and my children Akshay, Jayanth, Isha, and Dhrriti for believing in me. I am grateful for their constant support and encouragement.

Thank you to my adorable grandson Prayansh for saying, " Dadi aap kya kar rahe ho." "Dadi ko disturb mat karo." Life is so lovely with you around.

GOD BLESS EVERYONE

INDEX

1. BE HUMAN

Help yourself – Stay self-motivated

We are all gifted to be born as human beings; treasuring and valuing this valuable gift of the Almighty by preserving the qualities that make us different from other animals is the least we can do... Be Unique... But Be Human!

I would like to share a very inspiring story of a young girl named Poorvi. A great example compels us to believe that help comes when one wants to help oneself.

When youngsters get stuck in their problems, they tend to compromise in the given situation. All they need is a little support and care to help them come out of it and progress. But, either the youngsters are reluctant to share their problems with others, or even elders are hesitant to share their actual experiences. They do this probably to maintain a special image in front of the young. At times, because of the previous notions of the youngsters, the youngsters tend not to share their problems, thinking that the elders will only either ridicule them or scold them or may shrug them off because it's a trivial thing that needs no worry.

Let us now see how the situations shared by one and heard by the other do not remain the same when handled with love, care, and trust.

Poorvi was a very creative, talented, and hardworking girl, and in line with her attributes, she got a job in an advertising company that she had always dreamt of. She was cautious enough first to absorb the culture of the advertising agency. Since she was very passionate about her work, it was natural that it reflected in the outcome of the presentations she made.

When she was confident she could make a tangible contribution to the company, Poorvi decided to discuss her innovative ideas with her boss… little knowing that she was inviting trouble in her life for the years to come.

Some people keep their insecurities ahead of the company's well-being, and so did her boss do so. He quickly figured out that Poorvi was good but would soon be a threat to him as her work spoke volumes. To not allow that at any cost, her boss started tactics like insulting, abusing, and discouraging her whenever she tried to present her ideas. To the extent that when Poorvi put forward her presentation, everyone present there gave a loud applauding except her boss. Instead, he would provide irrelevant negative feedback to discourage her.

Creativity quickly gets dampened when not nurtured… and this is what exactly happened to Poorvi. Preserving her well-paid job was also a priority as she needed to support her family. Since she was able to manage ends well, she never looked for a new job. Slowly her interest, creativity, zest, innovative ideas, etc., started dying down, and so did her health. She was barely the Poorvi that she was when she had joined her job.

Soon she was married to Dinesh, who belonged to a friendly family. Poorvi had the liberties to live her life the way she wanted…. no restrictions whatsoever. Things were well on track and under control. Poorvi, the diligent person she was, earned all the love, respect, and recognition from her in-laws, too… but Poorvi still felt a vacuum in herself.

As a woman, it isn't challenging to understand the other woman. Damyanti, Poorvi's mother-in-law, observed the dissatisfaction in Poorvi's eyes and decided to talk to her. She wanted to know the cause of concern and so began with the process of elimination. Damyanti began by asking Poorvi about her married life. Since Poorvi was happy, she had lots of positive and happy thoughts. Slowly, Damyanti moved to Poorvi's work life. Initially, she shared positive instances but slowly poured her heart out about the discontentment she felt from within as she hadn't been doing things the way she intended to … her creativity had never been allowed to spread wings!!

After speaking her heart out, Damyanti gave her a glass of water and made a nice cup of tea for both. They both sipped the hot tea and relaxed a bit; after Poorvi calmed down completely, her mother-in-law asked whether she would like to hear a real story?

Since Poorvi was tired of speaking and was sipping her favorite masala tea, she nodded her head. At least she knew that the story she was about to listen to would bring a big twist and turn to her existing life.

Her mother-in-law started narrating…

A young girl was a very carefree, bubbly, lively, and happy-go-lucky type. If there were social media, she would have a huge friend list in those days. She graduated, got married, and had two lovely children. Her husband was a gentleman, but his family culture, values, and lifestyle were very different… opposite from where this girl's family and life. She was married into a conservative family, and speaking or even sparing a smile to anyone was not appreciated, and rather strictly prohibited. It was like a massive shock to this little young lady. Nonetheless, being what the family wants you to be is taught to the girls in the society; happy yet dissatisfied, this lady leads a life as it is for years. Further in life, due to some untoward incidences, the family started facing a financial crisis; she necessitated to look for a job because of such adversity.

She stepped into the teaching profession. It was her first job—the so-called NOBLE PROFESSION.

On the very first day of work in a school, after years, she had stepped into a very different environment. Her school, like every school, was vibrant, lively, and a happy place. As colleagues and students shared pleasantries, teachers exchanged ideas and shared their classroom experiences …. In short, this lady was in a space that brought her back into an atmosphere she was in when she was a child and a youngster. Though life circumstances had bogged her completely, she retorted to step out to work…despite all adversities-She Was Happy And Felt Alive That Day And After That!!!

Her inner self took a sigh of relief. She thanked God for rekindling the 'Real Her' … again!!!

Damyanti now asked Poorvi, "do you wish to know whose real-life story was it?" Poorvi quickly said, "yes, why not." Damyanti said, "this is my own real-life story."

Poorvi jumped out off the sofa and said, "REALLY?" The lady nodded.

Damyanti told Poorvi that this family was not the way it is now. The changes happened gradually…in fact, after being struck

                               Stepping into their shoes

by adversity.

Poorvi got near her and hugged her.

Damyanti said, "When our inner self agrees to one thing and the world forces you to do something else, you are going wrong." If one cannot change the place, they must try to create an opportunity that agrees with the inner self.

These were the words that helped Poorvi recapitulate her entire life!! She realized what had transpired in her life and how she had lost her authentic self. She appreciated that her mother-in-law was the one because she has such a lovely environment at home, and now it's time she works for a better atmosphere at the workplace.

Damyanti advised Poorvi to plan for a better life.

Poorvi thanked God for this transforming moment.

Poorvi worked on starting up her advertising agency. She put up her resignation papers to the utter surprise of her boss and other colleagues.

Poorvi formed a team of dedicated, self-driven, creative members. She got a platform and provided her teammates with a platform to showcase their talent and help grow the company.

Soon Poorvi's company gained the name and fame that she had always expected and dreamt of each passing day. Her steadfast dedication, devotion, and discipline helped her reach that level... which helped her regain her authentic self.

The takeaway in Poorvi's words-"Wait for the right time. We need to have patience. Let the ray of light, or we can say that 'Self-motivation', sustain within you.

To summarise, I believe we need to try and connect with

the right people or just analyze our situation, be our judge, stay cautious, make intentional decisions in life, accept responsibilities with ease, and live life to the fullest. Our help is just a step ahead."

My takeaway from this story is- Never lose hope in life, stay self-motivated, and have patience; your time is a vital thought ahead.

(As said to me by Ms. Poorvi)

LIFE IS PRECIOUS AND BEAUTIFUL
'IT'S TIME TO LIVE AGAIN'

Stepping into their shoes

2. Be Positive. Negativity Is Harmful

It's the attitude that takes you where you are

Sometimes, we fall into situations where we cannot handle ourselves and thus feel helpless in our lives. Even though we are well aware that keeping ourselves in the right state of mind is in our own hands, we get stuck in that situation and thoughts and cannot help ourselves come out of that whirlpool.

This story is of a patient who emerged from a life-threatening situation by understanding the true meaning of life. It helped him lead his remaining life very well planned, happy, and helping others in similar situations.

We should learn to lead our lives happily with a come what may attitude. Life unfolds each day with new problems and a bundle of solutions. Pick one key for each situation and keep moving. There is always help by our side, and we need to extend our hand to accept help.

Arun was happily married for ten years. He lived with his retired father, mother, wife, and son. But, he remained stressed about his family-his ageing parents, his son's education and higher studies, and his loving and caring wife's security since he was the sole breadwinner of his family. He ran short of money at times, but his wife managed the finances very well. She did her duties well. Overall, they were a happy family.

One day at work, Arun had a severe stomach ache and fell from his chair; the pain was unbearable. He was almost unconscious when taken to the nearby hospital. A concerned doctor did all the basic tests, and Arun gained consciousness after a few hours as he got a tranquilizer to lessen his pain. After the preliminary tests, the doctor suggested some further investigation. He also recommended another specialist from the same hospital.

Arun paid a visit to the doctor, Dr. Geeta. She was a pleasant old lady. Since she was very approachable, they soon were comfortable discussing Arun's case. She advised him to do some advanced tests. As fate had in store for Arun, he was diagnosed with intestinal cancer.

Knowing this, he almost lost hope of survival and was in despair. It is natural; he was more stressed than ever, given his circumstances. He would share his doubts, stressors, and anxiousness every day during his treatment. He saw no hope. He had almost given up the chance to survive, leaving aside from getting to everyday life. Though the doctor always gave him hope, he would tend to repeat the same lines:

a)Why did the Almighty choose him for this trouble?

b)How will the family survive without me?

c)I will die soon

d)There is no treatment for my sickness.

He never thought of all he could do to cure himself or come out of that negative zone. He got stuck in his negative thought process.

Dr. Geeta initially ignored it for a few days but soon realized that this might harm his mental health.

He would always cry in front of his family and show his helplessness. If the doctor tried to give him the strength, he would shrug her off, saying,

'You are talking like this because you have never faced such a situation ever in your life' and again started pitying himself. Dr. Geeta was apprehensive about Arun's mental health. She also knew everyone in his family by now. Rather than asking his family to take care of him, she thought of empowering Arun and redirecting his thought processes herself.

After spending some time with herself in her cabin, she returned to Arun and asked his permission to share something personal with him. Arun quickly agreed out of respect for the doctor who had been with him throughout these days.

With his permission, she started narrating her own life story. Arun could not understand why the doctor would tell her story to him. Anyways, he heard her story with full attention.

She said, "I had stones in my gall bladder. My husband and I had been aware of it since the birth of my younger son. But we kept postponing the surgery as it was not bothering me and was not an emergency. Firstly, my children were small, and there was no one to take care of them. Secondly, my father-in-law was bed-ridden. My mother-in-law was in depression and was in terrible shape too. I was the only caretaker of the entire family; I could not take proper care of myself. Days passed, and months and years went by, but we couldn't find a time slot to go for surgery. Whenever my husband asked me about my health, I would assure him that I was doing fine.

Eventually, after almost twelve years, we planned to get my surgery done. My kids were big enough to take care of themselves, and unfortunately, I lost both my father and mother-in-law within these years.

We made an appointment with the doctor, got all the required tests done, and planned the surgery after a fortnight.

A day before the surgery, I saw a small lump on my left breast while taking a bath. I mentioned it to my husband, who is a heart surgeon. We did not waste even a single day and completed all the required tests. The mammography and ultra-count also happened. The radiologist must have seen something as she told me to get the FNAC test done. She repeated the test twice to be sure. The next day we got the reports and knew that it was breast cancer. My husband was in a state of shock. He got shattered. We had planned so many things that we had to do in life.

But strangely, I was not afraid and thought this to be yet another trouble in our lives. I consoled my husband by saying do not lose heart, and I will be fine and live the life as we have always expected. I will handle it all and be back to my routine very soon. I knew that my family would be shattered and scattered if I gave up. We went to another specialist and got operated on. My husband was still low but gained his strength after looking at my willpower.

One fine day, my husband decided to explain my health condition to our children as they should also understand what their mother was going through.

My husband used to break down seeing me in pain, but, as usual, I always used to appease him. Though in pain, I was the backbone of my family. I did not let anyone cry about my condition. I wanted to work more for all the people in similar pain and be a motivation to them.

I went through all the pain, processes, and treatment you are going through now. I was too shallow during the treatment process, but deep in my heart, I knew that I had to go back home to my children and husband and live in this beautiful world for a long time.

When I look back, I realize that I used to be uncomfortable in specific postures while lying down but ignored everything, thinking that nothing could happen to me. And the thought of this trouble never popped up in my mind. I was neither obese nor had a family history of anything like that. By God's grace, blessings of all elders, and best wishes of my friends, I could heal properly. It took time to come back to my routine, but I took it as a challenge and see, now I am in front of you.

God gave me the courage and the right spirit at the right time. I was not at all conscious of losing my hair during Chemotherapy. I would instead cover my head with a scarf and socialize in my complex. My husband's support was tremendous. The lousy phase passed- thankfully. I deal with my life situations with great ease. I started motivating people to look at life positively despite the body's illness. I tell them - troubles help you realize that life is short, precious, and beautiful. So, live it to the fullest.

I thank God for this trouble because, from that day onwards, we as a family have never postponed things in life and give our best in the present. We learned to enjoy the gift of life and be happy… always. From that day onwards, the slogan of my life is - live life to the fullest.

I go for my regular check-ups, which have become a part of our routine. I am in front of you even after twenty years of that surgery.

No one in this hospital knows my story as I am new to this city. You are the first one in this city to know the reality of my life.

Initially, I hesitated to open up in front of you, but after looking at your attitude towards life and the harm you were causing yourself, I decided to share my story with you. We just have to look ahead in life and at the situation- treat it as a passing phase." She further told Arun, "you are young and will recover very fast. As your doctor, I can assure you. Regular care and a positive attitude is all you need. Assure yourself and then your family that you are coming back home and will get back to work very soon."

Dr. Geeta made Arun realize that he was not the only one who had faced something like this. She made him realize that rising above all hardships of life is the only way to lead life. We have to respect life, no matter how long or short it is. Nobody knows the day, date, and time of one's death, so we are no one to decide when to leave this world.

Dr. Geeta's story relieved Arun's mental stress. He now faced the process of his treatment with great courage. He conveyed to his family that he is a strong person, and with their love, blessings, and good wishes, he will recover soon and be back to his daily routine and work like before. He also gave them the example of his doctor. Though the chemotherapy sessions were challenging for him, he gained back his strength once that was over. He became more particular about things and enjoyed every moment of his life.

He was thankful to his doctor, who helped him with the proper physical and mental treatment when he needed it the most. He had more happy times with his family than ever before and valued every moment of life. He motivated people around him to relax and enjoy the beautiful gift of life.

In Arun's words, "We all are blessed with human life, and

all the problems are part and parcel of this life. It is up to a person how to handle it. It is always good to have that positive attitude to maintain peace and happiness. Had my doctor not told her life incident to me with so much clarity, it would have been difficult for me to handle and lead my life so wonderfully."

My takeaway is -Life puts you into many troubles time and again, we have to keep moving and embracing the problems with our bundle of solutions. It is well said that every problem comes with its solution. The sooner we find the right one for us, the more prepared we are for the next one. Every turbulent time has to end.

(As said to me by Arun)

LIFE IS PRECIOUS AND BEAUTIFUL

'IT'S TIME TO LIVE AGAIN'

Stepping into their shoes

3. The Habit of Being A Perfectionist

Make habits your slave; don't become a slave to habits

We come across people trying to become perfect, and it often leads to hindering their personal growth, relationships, and health, and they aren't able to enjoy life.. the actual purpose of life!

Stepping into their shoes

Here I would like to introduce you to a lady named Sonali who fell into deep trouble because of her habit…habit of doing things by herself and that too flawlessly. She shared her real-life experience- where she suffered a lot but learned her lesson too!

Sonali was a homemaker. Her kids were small, and she used to take good care of them as all mothers do. Her children scattered their toys around and spilled food and snacks here and there, as if every corner was their place to do whatever they wanted. Sonali, the dotting mother, always ran from corner to corner, clearing their mess as she couldn't tolerate anything out of place. She was proud of this attribute and often boasted about the same.

But naturally, people were wonderstruck by her and praised her for her efficiency, which Sonali thoroughly enjoyed and was satisfied with.

Sonali always wanted that appreciation, and she was getting it. She never realized that hidden in the corner of her head was that habit of perfectionism, and her ego was getting boosted. All this had already started taking a toll on her, but she ignored it. On the other end, she barely realized that her family was dependent on her- she had never trained her family members to be independent. Even her husband wasn't allowed to do anything as she felt he was tired after a long day at work. Her standard of cleanliness was so high that often maids too were reluctant to work for her. Cleaning the house, taking care of her kid's clothes, etc., was an uphill task.

Anything out of limit is definitely to give up, and so was Sonali's health…and one day, she opened her eyes in a hospital bed…

When she came to her senses, she saw her husband standing next to her and her arm plastered. He told her that she had collapsed while working in the kitchen. When the doctor came, he advised her to reduce the stress burden she had been living with and warned her of the potential problems she could fall into -physically and mentally. She was unable to respond due to weakness, drowsiness, and the effect of heavy doses of medicines.

A few days went by, and lying down on the bed, Sonali was alone talking to her inner self. Her subconscious mind was overactive at that time. Suddenly, she heard a voice. 'Hey slave'– she turned to see who was saying this to her. There was nobody around. She heard the words again and turned back again. Still, she could not find anyone when she realized that her inner self was talking to her. Sonali questioned herself, 'how am I a slave?' – The answer was not to be found.

Lying on the hospital bed, having all the medicines and injections, time and again, she kept worrying about what all she had to do when she got back home. She used to ask many questions from her husband and tell him what to do at home. He always answered, "do not think much, Sonali, just get well soon."

Old habits die hard, so she instructed the housekeeping staff to do the job better even while in the hospital. She would scream and abuse the lady named Chandrika for not cleaning the corners of the room and not doing this and that. That lady used to smile every time and do as she said. Every day, she pointed out some new mistake, and Chandrika would tolerate it with a smile.

It had already been ten days, and she was still in the hospital. As usual, on the tenth day, when Chandrika entered the room, Sonali had her list of complaints and instructions ready.

Chandrika calmly heard all her complaints and said with immense peace, ' Madam, you are correct in whatever you are saying, but, Can I ask you a few questions?' Sonali raised her brow but nodded her head in consent.

Chandrika asked – "Is your house clean?"

Sonali said, "What kind of question is this?"

Chandrika said, "I asked whether your house is clean right now or not?"

Sonali said, " Hmmm, I don't know."

Chandrika further added, "Where are your children?"

Sonali's answer was, "I don't know. Maybe, at home or …."

Chandrika asked, "Are they nourished hygienically?"

Are they doing their homework?"

Etc. etc.

Sonali had no answer to Chandrika's questions as she was not there where she was supposed to be. She was in the hospital instead.

Chandrika further said, "Sorry to say, but more than healing your body, you need to work on your mind…. The job is completed well only if it is your way is not the right way to think. Trust that others also know to do their job and that each one will do it with sincerity!"

She told her to introspect, " why not others but only she, i.e., Sonali, lying here sick in bed?" She further said, "Thinking yourself to be the best is good, but others are equally good, and so are their ways of leading life. We are no one to comment on them." Chandrika also sternly added, "Sorry to say, but you are the slave of your habit and see where you have reached."

This line hit Sonali hard as her inner self had constantly been repeating these words. Chandrika further said, "You should rather do the work within limits as your health permits and not impose your working style on anybody. Cultivating good habits is always appreciated, but it is useless if the habit leads to such ends."

Nobody had ever said something like this to Sonali!! She was constantly hurting her ego, but Sonali somehow liked how she initiated the conversation.

Chandrika continued, "We live life once. So have a healthy and happy life, not an agitated one. I do not mean that you should stop being neat and clean but let go of certain things beyond your boundaries. Be happy and spread happiness and also stay healthy. You are not only making your life miserable but also the life of people who are around you. Be thankful to the people who are taking care of your home now in their way and allowing you to be the way you are. Have gratitude for them. Try and appreciate their ways too."

	Stepping into their shoes

The more significant impact of her talks happened when Chandrika shared one of her life-changing instances, which taught Sonali a lesson for life.

Chandrika said that she once owned a housekeeping agency wherein she had several people working under her. Sonali was shocked and sat to hear her. Giving the best service to her clients was her motto, and for this reason, she was appreciated for her work. To continue gaining fame, she was too strict with her staff. Having food on time or calling it a day wasn't a part of her routine as contracts poured in from all sides. Chandrika said it was my Way or No way" system. My staff and I were stressed and overworked. I used to teach them my ways which, at times, were tedious and challenging for them.

As fate had in store, one day after having a long working schedule, Chandrika shared that she started feeling uneasy, and while coming down from her first-floor office, she fell from the staircase. She was unconscious for three days, and when she woke up, her body felt partially paralyzed. She could not work for months, and since her office was on loan, she could not repay the bank and was left in bed bankrupt.

A few months after recovering a little, this hospital in-charge was kind enough to give her a job as housekeeping personnel." Chandrika said, "she was thankful to them for offering her this job; at least, she could begin earning again. Chandrika added that her ego was shattered and her health too. She learned her life lesson to take care of herself and her work. We must know where to draw the line."

Chandrika's story shook Sonali mentally. It came as a huge shock.

She was listening to Chandrika and staring at her throughout. She never realized when Chandrika left the room. Sonali was in her world of thoughts. Sonali counted her blessings that she hadn't reached as bad a state as Chandrika. She realized where and when she had made mistakes and started planning how to improve herself in her imagination...

The moment she came out of her deep thoughts, she called Chandrika and touched her feet. Sonali thanked her for guiding her before it was too late. Sonali realized that one should cultivate good habits but being a slave to them is seriously not recommended. We should be cautious. This incident made her humble. After returning home, she started appreciating everyone and stopped instructing them. She began giving responsibilities to her family members. Though it was not easy for her and the family, in due time, all of them learned to change themselves for the better.

Sonali stays grateful to Chandrika, who was kind enough to share her life experience. She chose the right time to guide her when she was receptive to follow her guidelines. Sonali was thankful to her for making her life easy, happy, and healthy.

The takeaway in Sonali 's words –"We need to learn from everyone to improve ourselves. The kind of mistakes that we make in ignorance should be corrected. We don't have to learn only after our failure. It is better to stay alert and watch oneself have 'A Great Today' and 'An Even Better Tomorrow'. Being perfect is good, but being healthy is a must- people can give you a helping hand but can't give their health to you."

My takeaway is- Change yourself the moment you realize your mistake; you will feel relieved, liberated, and at peace!!!

(As said to me by Sonali)

LIFE IS PRECIOUS AND BEAUTIFUL
'IT'S TIME TO LIVE AGAIN'

Stepping into their shoes

4. Nature Understands Only Affirmative Lines

We have to be very specific about what we want in life. Our wishes come true. We have to think good to let good manifest.

This incident is about a retired government official Anand, who got help from a young guy Parijat. Unknowingly Parijat was instrumental in changing Anand from being an extremely rigid, unsatisfied, and stern person to a very happy-go-lucky person for the rest of his life.

Learning can happen at any age and from any generation. At times, the young adults set an example to an elderly adult unknowingly. One has to be receptive and open to learning the right thing and changing oneself for good. After all, life is a beautiful journey of failure, success, new learnings, and new beginnings.

Anand was an extremely disciplined person who had recently retired. But retirement didn't change his routine. He continued to be an early riser, go for walks and spend his day in a fixed practice. He had been preparing himself for retirement a few months before his retirement day. He proudly spoke about his post-retirement life plans in his retirement day speech. He already knew how to occupy himself post-retirement for the hours he used to spend in the office.

Things were pretty standard in Anand's life. Everyone around him thought so other than he!

Somehow, he had an undying nature of recollecting all those things that didn't materialize with him… things like, if in the past, he had gone to buy a watch of his choice, the shopkeeper would say that it was out of stock and doesn't know when it will be available again. If ever he wanted to buy a particular shirt, someone else would just pick it up before he reached the shop.

If ever he planned to go somewhere and queued for the railway ticket, the seats would be complete just before he reached the counter.

He had made a chain of his undone things in life and feared having any new wish- as he was confident it wouldn't materialize and remain unfulfilled.

His friends used to tell him about similar incidents, but he would insist that he is unlucky and that such things happen to him because of his ill fate. He had a bucket list of incomplete wishes, but he was sure that he would not be able to fulfill his desires. This belief of his made him frustrated and irritable by nature. Because of this reason, his friends started avoiding his company. Again, he blamed his fate.

Eventually, he used to go for morning walks all alone.

During his walk, he used to see a group of boys who did their morning exercise together and sat for some time for a healthy talk. Whenever Anand crossed them, he always wanted to be a part of this happy-go-lucky group, never believing it would happen.

It was a bright Sunday morning, and as usual, people were walking and jogging around in the garden. Anand, too, was there walking as usual. Unfortunately, there was a big stone on his path that he didn't notice, and he tripped and fell over. Seeing this, a group of people rushed to him. Anand couldn't get up to stand as he had sprained his ankle. Two boys volunteered and dropped Anand at his house. They offered to call the doctor, but Anand preferred calling his family doctor.

The doctor advised some medicines and asked him to take rest for a couple of weeks.

A week later, on a pleasant Sunday morning, one of the boys named Parijat, who had helped Anand back home, came to see him. Anand told him that he was better but suggested resting for a few more days before he could go out for walks.

Anand offered Parijat a cup of tea which Parijat willingly accepted. Both of them sipped the hot tea and started talking to each other. Parijat was one from the same group which Anand had observed and yearned to be a part of. Parijat was kind of enjoying his chat with Anand. Anand shared a lot about himself…he told him about his family, government job, and life post-retirement. As his nature, Anand also expressed his dissatisfaction about his wishes not getting fulfilled.

Anand mentioned that he never wanted a government job but had to do it due to family pressure. He never wanted to send his daughter to a Hindi medium school but had to do so. Anand never wanted to get his daughter married in a different caste but had to do it, as it was her choice. He never wanted to settle down in a small city but had to.

Anand also shared the small things that he could not get in life. After his retirement, he had his bucket list but was sure it won't come true. He also shared a few things from his list with Parijat.

Finally, he cared to inquire from Parijat as to what has Parijat been doing in life… personally and professionally.

Parijat introduced himself as an entrepreneur who liked adventure and fitness. When Parijat heard about Anand's bucket list, he asked Anand's permission to share one of his life experiences and assured Anand that he would fulfill his bucket list if he stopped talking more about his past. He requested Anand to forget about the past because the past is gone forever, and it will create a barrier in his present life.

Anand willingly agreed and started listening to Parijat's life experience.

Parijat said, "I had heard about para gliding from one of my friends and sub consciously got attracted towards it. Once, we were planning our vacation, and this thought popped up. Somehow, the break did not materialize, and my para gliding dream remained unfulfilled.

Whenever I heard someone planning an adventure vacation, I would always suggest them go para gliding. I had no idea that I was indirectly attracting things to myself. I used to be very happy if someone shared their para gliding experience - the thrill, the joy with me.

It so happened that I had to go to a hill station for some work for a couple of days. It was work and only work on my mind. I did not have any idea that I had already reached the place where my dream would come true. Even after so many canceled trips, I was in the place where I could fulfill my dream. The moment I reached the spot and entered the hotel, I saw people coming back from some adventure act and discussing their experiences with each other. They seemed to be so happy. Being an adventure enthusiast, I pushed myself to ask one of them which sport they were talking

Stepping into their shoes

about so excitedly. I was surprised and had goose bumps when I heard the name para-gliding. Now I realized that even if I was suggesting the thing to someone else all the time, I was attracting it towards me as well.

At times, I used to doubt the fulfillment of my wishes, but the only difference was that I never thought of not being able to do it. I just suggested it to all my friends and thought of doing it myself someday.

Soon I found some spare time after work and went for para gliding myself …When I was doing it, I enjoyed every moment, and the day seemed blissful!

I was trying to analyze why and how this thought materialized so fast within my heart. The only idea that came was that I never thought negatively about this experience this time.

I assured myself always to think positively and be optimistic in the core of my heart. We should look forward to enjoying and relish every moment of our life. We should learn from every experience and keep improving. There is a slimline between the type of thing we are attracting towards ourselves and what we want."

Parijat further suggested to Anand, "Uncle, please try this technique from now onwards to make your list of things to be fulfilled soon. You will surely feel the change within yourself. Even in our deep thoughts, we keep attracting things. Now onwards, do give a positive direction to your thoughts. Uncle, sometimes we keep saying I don't want this but end up getting that. You got what you want minus the 'not' word. After having this experience, I analyzed the type of thoughts that I had before this experience. I could say that I always had an unfinished wish whenever I used the word 'not.' If we add not to our sentence, the situation happens in a negative form. The law of attraction works at all times. Now, I can easily differentiate between them. We have to be very specific about what we want in life. It may not be a long-term goal all the time. It may be as small as wanting to eat ice cream.'

Parijat smiled and asked for Anand Ji's permission to leave and thanked him for the refreshing cup of tea. He also wished him good luck in fulfilling his bucket list and good wishes for his speedy recovery.

Anand thanked him with a smile as if this young fellow came to his house to give him a ray of hope. Anand felt a lot of positivity talking to Parijat. Anand was sitting in the same place for a while as he went deep into his thoughts to identify where he went wrong. It was happening for the first time with him.

One by one, the thoughts started rolling down. Anand realized that he was very negative in his approach to his wishes. He finally decided that rather than repenting for the days gone, he should at least have a positive path for the days and years to come.

He first stopped saying 'no' to things. He made an order of his wishes and started systematically planning them. He started framing affirmative sentences to his wishes. He observed that his wishes were elevating, and above all, he was happier than ever before.

After completing his first pilgrimage- his first wish on his bucket list-Anand desperately wanted to meet Parijat and thank him. He immediately got ready for his morning walk and approached Parijat. Parijat was busy exercising with his friends. Anand waited till he got done and then went near him and thanked him.

Anand was so happy that he could not put his excitement

                    Stepping into their shoes

into the right words. He became a child in front of Parijat. Though Parijat was very young and Anand was like a father to him, Anand profusely thanked Parijat for all the changes and positivity he was experiencing.

As Anand slowed down, he said, "you have completely changed my life and thought process. My family and friends are so happy with me now, and so am I. I fulfilled my first wish on my bucket list as I started having a positive approach toward what I wanted in life. Thank you for guiding me at the right time. God bless you."

Parijat never knew that just by sharing a little experience, he could change an elderly and experienced person like Anand Ji to this extent- that too, because they barely knew each other and over and above the age difference. The lovely soul he was, Parijat thanked the Almighty for choosing him to change someone's attitude towards life.

In Anand's words, his takeaway is that "It is not always about the age but the zest to learn that helps us improve in life and be happy. All those who are stuck in their unsatisfied life, this story would surely be a bright ray of hope to them."

My takeaway from this story is -Always be positive and attract likewise.

(As said to me by Anand)

LIFE IS PRECIOUS AND BEAUTIFUL
'IT'S TIME TO LIVE AGAIN'

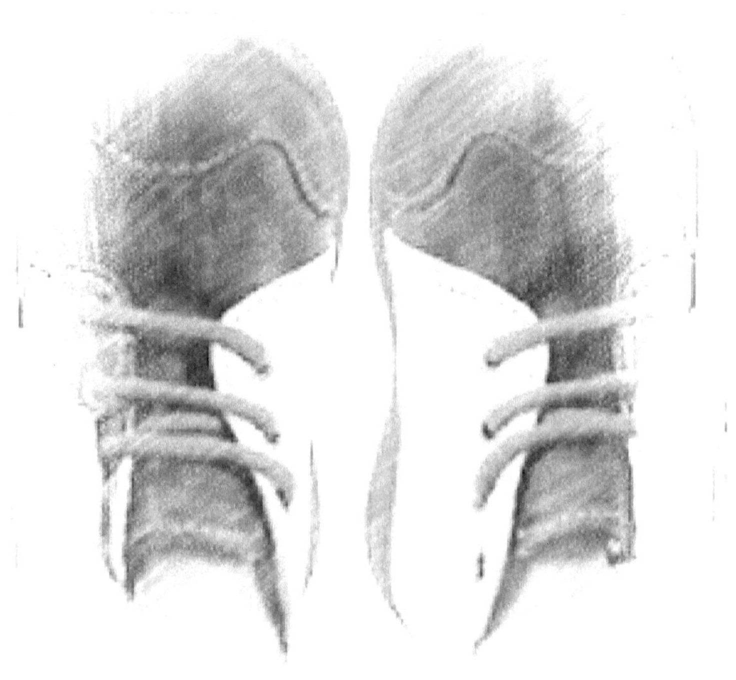

Stepping into their shoes

5. FIND YOUR HIDDEN TALENT

At times, we are busy doing things, but our inner self wants to do something else... we hardly heed it. More than often, ignoring this natural want from within makes us unhappy and reflects in our behavior which isn't in our control as we aren't aware; why?

It is a story of two lovely ladies called Sunita and Rohini. It's a great example that tells us how one woman can be a support system to the other and help realize their inner worth, inner self, and happiness.

Rohini was an old but young dance teacher and a thrilled-go-lucky person. She loved meeting people who were creative and fun-loving and, at all times, avoided people who involved themselves in baseless gossip.

Rohini shared with us a story about a very dear friend of hers.

Sunita was a hard-working, sincere, and good secondary school teacher. While teaching, most of her examples came from nature, plants, and especially flowers. She was popular among the students, parents, and colleagues for her innovative approach to academics. But, she had temper issues and often fought with her family members. After the fight, she would repent, but again, fight.

Rohini met Sunita at a friend's party. Though Sunita was relatively younger than Rohini, they both grew fond of each other as they gelled well. They started meeting each other on weekends as those were the only days when they were free. Sunita always appreciated Rohini's calmness and talent, and similarly, Rohini had all appreciation for Sunita as a good teacher.

Rohini related an instance. She said, "Once we went to a famous florist to buy a bouquet for our familiar friend's birthday. We entered the shop and started finding a pleasing fragrance. The moment I would select one, Sunita would find flaws in its arrangement. Sunita soon began fighting with the florist for making such dull and bad bouquets. She gave alternatives that could have given the aroma a better look.

After a prolonged argument with Sunita, the owner gave up and challenged her to make a better bouquet. She quickly accepted the challenge. We were already getting late for the party, but I thought of waiting for some more time since I knew about her love for flowers. The world of flowers drew Sunita's attention! She did not even realize that they were getting late. But, as guessed, she soon was ready with a vibrant and colorful bouquet that looked just right and beautiful.

All the people present at the shop were astonished, i.e., the florist, the staff, and the customers all clapped for the fantastic bouquet Sunita had made. Sunita thanked everyone for the compliments and came out of the shop happily and proudly carrying the bouquet that she had made herself.

At the party, I realized that Sunita seemed a different person. She was thoroughly enjoying the party. All the attendees appreciated the bouquet made by her... she was the center of attention, and Sunita enjoyed every bit of it."

Two days later, Sunita called Rohini and mentioned that the florist had called and requested her to make a few bouquets for him as the people present in the shop that day wanted the same kind of bouquet she had made. He also said that he would pay her for making those bouquets. She was confused about whether to accept his offer or not. Sunita sounded happy but confused.

Rohini requested Sunita to meet her for some time in the evening. She agreed. When they met, Rohini requested her to listen to her story. She happily agreed because whenever both of them met, Sunita was the one who used to talk more and express herself more. Rohini hardly spoke. Sunita felt very happy because this time, Rohini wanted to share something.

Rohini said that "a few years back, as a home maker, I always used to test and try new ways of cooking, loved decorating my house, was consistently well dressed and had a natural hand of class in whatever I did and loved the way I was.

I was a music lover. I used to relax and listen to music and sing along. Another thing that used to take its head up, time and again, was listening to dance numbers. Songs would make me close my eyes, and different people in colored costumes would start dancing with new and innovative dance steps. Though little trained in Kathak dance form, I noticed that the dance movements in my imagination were not just bound to kathak. I barely engaged in dancing except for a jig with my kids.

One day, one of my friends was in a fix because her daughter wanted to participate in her school dance competition. She expressed her helplessness because she couldn't find a good dance teacher in her vicinity. I assured her that I would soon find a good dance teacher for her.

Two days later, I received a call from that amicable, and

before she could say anything, I sincerely apologized that I, too, couldn't find her a dance teacher. My friend said that this call was an invitation to her daughter's birthday.

That evening we were all on the dance floor dancing to songs one after the other.

I didn't even realize it when I held the hand of the birthday girl. Helped her to use her feet and hands according to the rhythm.

Suddenly, I was lost in a different world and realized the hidden instinct of teaching dance and choreography. It came as a wave within me. The girl was also enjoying a lot of dancing with me. The music stopped, and we went for the cake cutting and snack time. All of us wished for the girl and enjoyed every moment of the party. That blessed day became an awakening day for me as my life changed after that. Before leaving the party, I approached my friend, saying that I would prepare her daughter for the dance competition.

My journey as a choreographer began from there. A few days later, the sweet little girl came to me with a twinkle and a spark in her eyes and said, 'Aunty, I won the competition.' I was so happy and thrilled that tears started rolling down. I was pleased about her success. I was also delighted to put the dance steps of my imagination into practical form!!"

"After that, there was no looking back. I started teaching whatever I knew, and students started pouring in. I soon started my dance academy. And here I am in front of you as you know me. I am delighted that I followed my intuition, instinct, and passion and earned from it, and above all am happy with what I am doing."

Sunita was astonished to listen to Rohini's story and soon agreed to work for the florist for a couple of hours every evening.

                                   Stepping into their shoes

Her bouquets were appreciated and became famous. She started getting more and more orders for the same. Apart from this, a significant change happened because she was calmer and a better person who barely got angry, and fighting was not a part of her personality anymore! All of us were extremely happy to see this transformation, and so was her family.

Sunita soon became a partner in that business and earned more than before. Everyone started calling her a 'florist teacher.' She was pleased with her new name and work. She was thankful to have met me, and I encouraged her toward a positive change.

She became a firm believer and left no chance to encourage others to try and find one's hidden talent as each one has at least one. Pursuing one's hidden talent allows us to live life to the fullest."

She propagated the message – 'Help yourself find that quality within yourself and prosper in life as I did.'

Take away in Rohini's words is- 'try to find out that hidden quality which is meant for our peace and happiness. Do not wait for a Rohini to inspire you, Be your own Rohini. Each one is blessed with a unique and exceptional talent…all one needs to do is delve into the new opportunities that seem morally right yet exciting.

My take away from this instance is that we need to properly recognize and nourish our creativity and talent as it becomes a significant reason for our happiness.

(As said to me by Rohini)

LIFE IS PRECIOUS AND BEAUTIFUL
'IT'S TIME TO LIVE AGAIN'

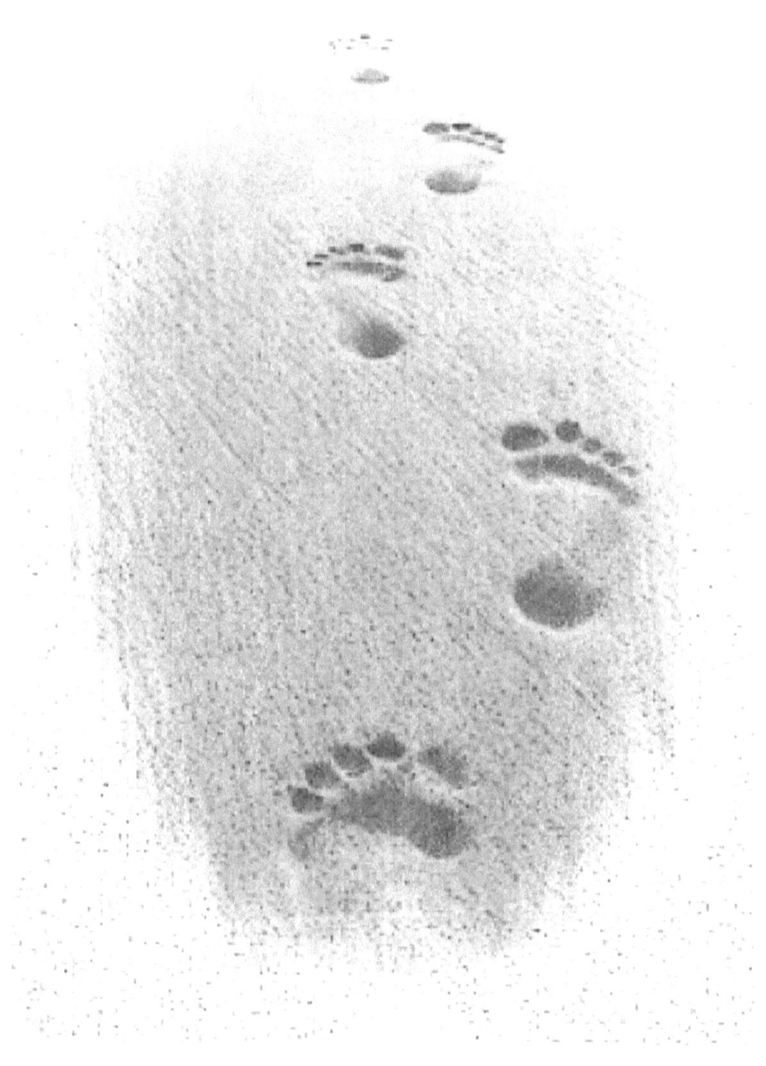

Stepping into their shoes

6. Me Time

A miraculous way to transform your life.

Starting and ending a day with a few minutes with yourself helps you to know yourself better and organize your day.

This story is of a village girl who married a guy belonging to a big city. She confuses herself with the new dos and don'ts of her new life and how she was helped by a spiritually inclined neighbor to adjust to the unique circumstances- shifting her from confusion to comfort.

If ever a person is stuck in an unwanted situation, we should remain calm. At that point-probably, help is around the corner- just open doors.

Ranu was a simple, joyous, and friendly village girl. Her father, also her best friend, raised her with all the love and attention. She had lost her mother when she was a toddler. She completed her studies and loved every corner of her lovely village. Never did Ranu aspire to go anywhere. But of course, her father thought differently. He knew that stepping and moving out to a different town would give his daughter a different experience …different exposure and…a different world.

Ranu's father's wish came true when an old friend asked for Ranu's hand for his son. The boy was working in an MNC in the city. Ranu's father trusted his friend and considered this the most suitable match for his loving daughter. Ranu did not have her own choice to get married, so she agreed to her father's choice. She did not even think twice as she trusted her father completely.

Held a simple wedding function, and the villagers wholeheartedly blessed the couple. Ranu had that bridal glow on her face.

Besides having a new friend as a life partner, Ranu hardly found it different after marriage. They went to a hill station for a few days to better know each other. It was the first time she had stepped out of her village.

It was almost a month when they stepped into the city, into her husband's house. To begin with, she was very excited to set up her new home with all new things. Setting up the house in the city was different from taking care of the house in the village. Ranu and her husband managed to do things well. He never pointed or said anything her way, as he understood that she was new to her surroundings and respected that. He believed she would slowly learn to adjust to the new lifestyle.

Ranu was also pleased to get so many new clothes. Every day she would wear a new dress and flaunt it in front of the mirror. She was a happy person.

Her father stayed in the village, and her in-laws lived in another city where they were working. Household work was not a big task for Ranu because she was used to taking care of everything in the village. Her husband was also fond of home-cooked food.

At times, she used to feel bad for her father, whom she had left alone in the village. Her father assured her that he would do all the work by himself and keep updating her about the same. He also

Stepping into their shoes

assured Ranu that he was magnificent and happy.

Things changed when her husband joined the office after a long vacation.

Whenever she moved out of the home with her husband, she used to be friendly with everyone. She moved quickly here and there as she did in the village. She would speak a little loud whenever in a group or while walking on the road, catching the people's attention around her. She had no clue why people stared at her and often wondered about the same. To sum it up, there was nothing wrong with her, only that her ways were different and not 'urban appropriate' as one may say. For the same reason, some looked and laughed at her. Some thought her to be illiterate and did not have manners or etiquette to behave in society.

Her actual test began when her husband asked her to behave in a specific manner all the time.

'Behave properly. What will people say?'

'These actions will give you a bad name in society.'

'Dress up like this.'

'Eat like this.'

'Speak like this.'

'Walk the way the society expects you to walk,'

and this & that and so on.

Her husband started instructing her.

Initially, she tried to adjust to the new ways taught to her, but soon she felt suffocated. Both of them loved each other, but due to these incidences...they were moving apart.

Though she tried her level best, Ranu still could not fix the urban lifestyle. She started missing her village life where she could be herself. Though there was a good understanding between Ranu and her husband, deep within herself, she had already started getting frustrated. Her husband loved her a lot and wanted her to change.

Gradually, her husband stopped taking her to group gatherings as he felt embarrassed, and even Ranu understood his limitations. She was trying her level best to change but in vain.

It was two years, and she was still unsettled… to add to her misfortunes, her father had expired. Now, the only person she had by her was her husband, and as we know, who didn't accept her the way she was. His parents were good to her but didn't or couldn't stay with them.

To keep up her and her husband's dignity she started recoiling and stayed alone at home throughout the day….

An older woman named Amrita Ji in their neighborhood used to observe Ranu. For all these years, all they did was exchange a smile when they came across.

One day Amrita Ji came to meet Ranu to offer her condolence on the sudden demise of her father. Amrita Ji was around 69 years of age, soft-spoken, sweet, and gentle. After that, they kept in touch and met often.

Gradually, Ranu started sharing her life experiences with Amrita Ji, which often made Amrita Ji go down memory lane.

One day both went for a walk. Amrita Ji, by now, had gauged that Ranu wanted to change herself but at the same time wanted to retain her identity and individuality. Amrita Ji asked Ranu, "can I share one of my life experiences?" Ranu happily agreed to it.

                                    Stepping into their shoes

She said, "it will be my pleasure to hear as I am the one who keeps talking all the time." Amrita Ji smiled and began.

She said, "Years ago when I was a child, my mother insisted that I spend a few minutes early in the morning before leaving the bed and at night before going to bed with myself.

She guided me to talk to myself – firstly, thank Our Creator for gifting me a new day and allowing me to do new things and plan the day.

Before going to bed, she guided me to thank the Almighty for the beautiful day again, recapitulate whatever I did during the day, and recollect whether I did the things according to what was planned. Also, what were my learnings from my deeds, analyze if I went wrong somewhere, to accept and learn from my mistakes. What good did I come across? And how can that be imbibed as a part of my life and so on?

I always used to begin and end my day on a very positive note.

All this became an inseparable ritual or a routine of my day. It has helped me a lot in my life. I am what I am just because I religiously followed this routine. I have learned from my mistakes. Accepting my mistake has become easy for me as I know this is for my betterment. Changing myself according to my situation and circumstance has become equally easy."

Amrita Ji looked into Ranu's eyes and said, "Now, Ranu, if you ever think that things have been very easy for me in life, then you are incorrect. You are not the only one who has faced problems. I have had my share of ups and downs in life. I was primarily thrown in a whirlpool of turbulent tides of wanted and unwanted situations in my life, but this habit helped me face it and come out of it with brilliance. Every change came as a challenge which I accepted quickly because of this daily routine. I have always thanked my mother for giving me this gift of life. Though she is no longer with me, her teachings always keep her alive in me.

Please, suggest you try and follow this routine for a few days if it works for you. If it does not work, you can quickly leave it and live the way you wish.

If my life experience can be of any help to you, then I will be thankful to the Almighty for this. If it starts helping, you will be well equipped to handle the so-called worldly problems of your life. You are just beginning the beautiful new phase of life called married life. You will eventually start enjoying your own company and never get bored of this beautiful life.

I have come across many people in this world who search for happiness. They go here and there but are still unhappy, or you may say that unhappiness becomes their comfort zone. They are unable to help themselves. Try and press the reset button before 'Staying Unhappy' becomes your lifestyle …

Spending time with yourself is like a boon to be happy and contented in this beautiful world. It has helped me remain positive, lively, happy, contended & cheerful in my life.

Being true to yourself is essential. Never pity yourself. It is all about accepting your mistake and overcoming it by changing yourself. Whatever you do in your life, talk to yourself and then step ahead. Your inner self is your best guide. If ever you are guilty of something, that deed is surely wrong.

This realization can happen if you are in the habit of talking and being in close contact with yourself, even if you get placed in a

Stepping into their shoes

situation where you work without interest. Sitting alone for at least ten minutes each day gives you the strength to analyze the situation. It also helps you to adjust well to that unwanted situations. It makes you strong. So, be with yourself for a few minutes, analyze your situation and work towards it."

Ranu was thrilled to listen to all this as she had already started experiencing a different outlook on life. She realized that Amrita Ji is filling the vacuum caused by her mother's absence in her life. She soon started practicing self-talk the way Amrita ji had guided her. She gradually became a happy person. She could feel the change of accepting the situation and finding out her way of dealing with them. She changed for good without losing her original self.

One significant change that she saw in herself was that she started speaking softly but never felt bad about it. She could clearly and precisely express herself. Speaking loud seemed exhausting to her. She realized that speaking loud was required in the village as people lived at a distance, unlike here in comparatively tiny apartments. She willingly started going to social gatherings with her husband.

She got all the encouragement and motivation from within. Above all, her husband encouraged her to pursue her studies which she happily accepted. She always wanted to become a doctor by profession. The day when Ranu got admission, she ran to Amrita Ji with a box of sweets to seek her blessings. Amrita Ji was like her mentor, who had put Ranu's life on a progressive and purposeful track. Further, in life, Ranu left no opportunity to share Amrita ji's technique so that more and more people could lead a happy and contented life. Ranu remains indebted to Amrita Ji.

Ranu's takeaway from this story was that she never thought that Amrita Ji was interfering in her life. Instead, she tried to learn her good practices and imbibe them. If youngsters start adopting such practices from their elders, the coming generation will surely be progressive. Similarly, Amrita Ji could have thought of making fun of Ranu or looking down on her, but instead, she shared the secret of happiness with Ranu, and Ranu shared it with many.

My takeaway from this incident is that consistently spending time introspecting and analyzing helps you improve, progress, and prosper in life!

(As said to me by Ranu)

LIFE IS PRECIOUS AND BEAUTIFUL
'IT'S TIME TO LIVE AGAIN'

                                          Stepping into their shoes

7. Be happy for what you are blessed with

Look into your plate

At times we do not realize and value what we have. We just love to remain unsatisfied. We always think that the other person has better things than us. They have a better life than us. On the contrary, we should count our blessings and feel good about others.

This incident is about a young college student named Ashish who always used to envy everyone around him. He would pity himself and never realize what good he has in life. He was also accommodating, humble, intelligent, and a sincere boy. This beautiful real-life story is how who and what incidents help him count his blessings.

With the help of this story, I pray that many would benefit and come out of their negative comfort zone and love the life they have.

Ashish was very good in his studies. He had everything that a person could dream of in his young days but always had excuses and justifications for his imaginary pitiful condition. He would portray himself as having a hard life…always crib. Ashish would find that one bad thing from the bundle of good things happening around him would cause his unhappiness. He used to be unhappy almost all the time.

One day, while returning home from college on a peddle rickshaw, Ashish met one of his close friends, Rohan. Ashish asked him to join him as both had to go the same way. Rohan willingly accepted and climbed up. On their way back, Ashish asked him whether he had finished writing his psychology notes or not. Rohan immediately said, 'yes, I have.' He further said, 'last night my younger brother was doing his project work and the lights were switched on till late night so I thought of completing my work too.'

Now Ashish got a reason to crib. He said, 'O… I wish I had a younger brother as you have. I could talk or study with him just like you. It would've been great help, but I don't know why God has given me all the problems. If I had company at home, I would have been the first one to finish my work. I have a hard time studying due to this reason. I have to sit in the college library to finish my work.' He went on and on and on.

Rohan just happily told Ashish about completing his work, but Ashish had to find the negative side of everything and pity himself. Rohan felt very bad about it and wanted to teach Ashish a lesson. The smile on Rohan's face lowered. Still, he kept on nodding his head to show his consent.

Suddenly, the peddle rickshaw entered a puddle, and both of them fell from the rickshaw. Though they did not hurt themselves much, Ashish started complaining about why something wrong always happened to him!!! He said that I have never hurt someone ever in my life, but all these troubles find me all the time. Ashish did not even realize that even Rohan had got hurt. He was sobbing and complaining about his pain.

On the contrary, Rohan asked the rickshaw puller whether he was ok or not. When the rickshaw -puller gave no as an answer, he also apologized for this negligence. Rohan just asked the rickshaw-puller to be careful next time as they were saved this time.

                                    Stepping into their shoes

After listening to these unusual talks of Ashish, Rohan got upset and wanted to tell Ashish that we should always count on one's blessings and not troubles. These kinds of incidents are just a part of our lives. Rohan said, 'don't worry, Ashish, we used to fall so many times even during childhood.' Rohan found the right time to help Ashish come out of this thought process but was not finding the right time.

This particular incident triggered Rohan to teach Ashish a lesson. He started speaking in a flow with an assertive voice. 'Dear friend, let us do one thing. Let us first exchange my brother with your father if you want what God has blessed me with. Ashish raised her brow and stopped cribbing over what had happened for a while. Rohan continued, 'you very well know that I lost my father when I was too small. Have you ever seen me uttering depressing words? I also want my father back. You always crib for small-small things, which is not good.'

'We should be happy with what God has given us and not how we want things to be. Why do you even have to see what the others have on their plate? Always? Look into your plate and be happy. Count on your blessings. Nobody in this world has all that they want. Everyone has got their share of good and bad things in life. I am your friend, and I must guide you right.

These lines would have helped Ashish come out of the zone of complaints. On the contrary, he got angry, got down from the rickshaw, and angrily moved into his house. Rohan's house was a little ahead, so he moved on. Ashish did not even wish Rohan before leaving. He got offended about why Rohan asked for his father in exchange for his brother. He acted foolishly, not understanding the hidden meaning of what his friend had just told him. He thought that Rohan was rude and did not know how to be polite and kind to his friend.

Ashish entered his home in haste, threw his bag on the side chair kept in the entrance of the first room, and ran to his room. His grandmother watched the whole scene from a big window near the door of their house. She was an old lady who loved Ashish a lot. After some time, she took a glass of water and entered Ashish's room. She slowly stepped in his room. Seeing his granny, he did not even want to have water since he was upset. He also asked his granny to leave him alone and leave his room.

She got a little upset with his behavior but silently kept the glass of water on the side table and left the room. She thought that Ashish must have fought with Rohan for some reason. She preferred leaving Ashish for some time – allowing 'his me time' to analyze the situation and come out of it on his own.

In the evening, when Ashish calmed down, he came to his grandmother and asked her to forgive him for his misbehavior. She agreed and said that she would forgive him only if he told her the reason for his anger. Ashish thanked his granny for understanding him and immediately decided to tell her the cause as he was very close to his grandmother.

Ashish's grandmother patiently heard the entire conversation between the two friends. She knew the cribbing habit of her grandson and hadn't found the right time to explain specific facts of life and how everything in life is precious. She analyzed the situation, consoled Ashish, and assured him to discuss it further after dinner. She always wanted Ashish to become a problem solver in life himself.

Ashish was a little surprised with her answer as his granny would always give her solutions immediately after listening to his problems. He thought maybe she was not taking his issue seriously.

He asked her why we couldn't discuss it now. She said it was time for her evening walk, and her friends were waiting for her.

Ashish reluctantly agreed and waited for that right time after dinner. He had always got convincing answers from his granny, so he thought it was worth waiting a few more hours.

After having dinner, Ashish came to his granny's room, sat next to her, and his granny began speaking the truth of her life, which non of the family members knew about it in detail.

She asked Ashish to listen to her carefully as she would tell her life story to him, believing that he was grown up enough to know and understand it. Ashish was eagerly waiting for an answer to his problem, but since he was very fond of his granny, he came close to her to hear about her life experience. Ashish thought he would ask about his problem after she finished her story. When she said that you are the first to know about this in the family in detail, Ashish was keener in listening to that secret of her life that no one knew. He had always seen his grandmother solving others' problems, and no one had heard her side of the story.

His granny said, "I was the only girl of my parents, and both loved me a lot. I grew up receiving all the good values that they taught me. We were not remarkably well-off financially but never felt the need to have anything more than what we had. My father taught me to be happy with whatever we have and make the best use of it. My mother used to teach me how we should accept life changes. We were a happy family. When I turned nine, there was a drastic change in my life. My parents fell ill with a disease called plague. I lost both of them at a very tender age. I was left alone with nobody to take care of me. I had never met any relatives ever. My mother and father were the only children of their parents, and both paternal and maternal grandparents expired before I was born. I never had the privilege of being with my grandparents. We were a delighted family and never felt the need to have anyone else with us.

I think we were in a rented house as a few days after my parents expired, a very kind lady came and put me in an orphanage. She must be the house owner, and I don't even remember her name or face. I was in that orphanage for a few years. I adjusted there well and adopted the ways of that orphanage. Initially, I used to miss my parents a lot but soon realized that everyone was an orphan. All of us had to learn to live without our parents. Though the head of the orphanage was a strict lady, she was very fond of me. I used to study alone with no support. In the orphanage, I used to do all the work as instructed to me. Though I used to feel lonely at times, I never let anyone know that and kept following my parents' teachings.

Once I completed my graduation, I started working as a school teacher. I did not discuss my life with anyone. Further, the orphanage people selected a groom for me, and I got married. Even your grandfather was an orphan, so we had too many things in common. We both soon adjusted to our circumstances. A few years later, I gave birth to a baby boy; he gave us immense happiness to both of us but, left us when he was two years old. We got shattered, and life was meaningless again. Soon, we welcomed another baby boy- your father. We started living our life looking at his innocent

                                      Stepping into their shoes

acts... We were a happy family.

When your father was five years old, I lost my husband in a train accident. Again, a significant setback for me. Still, I did not lose hope and became busy with my job and taking care of my son. Years and years passed, and I remember my parents and their teachings whenever I got in trouble. I always adjusted well to the present situation, thinking that it was the best God could give me. I never craved for what I did not have. I used to be happy with what I had and adapt to my circumstances. My adaptability bar had risen to a higher level.

Your father studied well and grew up to be a gentle person. He married the girl of his choice. They were a perfect couple. A few years after their marriage, they welcomed a son, that is you, Ashish. All of us never felt the need to discuss my life within the family as we trusted each other and understood the needs of each other. My previous life was of significantly less importance in my day-to-day life."

Ashish was quiet and patiently listening as if a film had rolled down in front of his eyes. But this time, it was a real story and not just a story. His grandmother further said, "Ashish, here I am in front of you, and you have known me ever since you gained senses."

Grandmother said, "when I saw you upset today in the afternoon. Then when you told me about your argument with Rohan, I aspired to share my life experience with you thinking that it might help you come out of your unsatisfied zone of this beautiful life. This life always has beautiful things to give you; it depends on you and what you pick. Life is a one-time offer given to you by the Almighty."

Granny further ended by saying, I just had this much to say. You may now go off to sleep as it is already too late."

Ashish did not say a single word to her. He just hugged her good night and left for his room. That night was the night of transformation. He recollected all the incidents his grandmother had faced and was still happy in her present situation. He appreciated her courage and attitude towards life.

Further, he went into the flashback of his life. He always cribbed for not having this or that and remained unsatisfied and troubled everyone around him, which now appeared small to him. He was emotional and sensitized about the life situations of his grandmother and everyone around him. He thought that his grandmother had to face so much in life, yet she was always happy. My father is always energetic in meeting all the challenging situations in life, even after losing his father early. My mother takes good care of us, and the house is complete, yet I have remained unsatisfied.

I SHOULD CHANGE MYSELF.

He slept thinking about all this.

The following day, he woke up happy and determined to change his perspective about life and reward himself with a gift of happiness. He hugged everyone and wished them good morning. It was an unusual but pleasant surprise for his family members. He thanked his grandmother for sharing her experience and told her that he understood her motive for telling her life experience to him. He also said, "I thank the Almighty for blessing you in my life." His grandmother hugged him with affection and said, "Now, my little boy is a grown-up boy." Both had a hearty laugh and hugged each other again. Ashish also requested her to help him time and

Stepping into their shoes

again with her tips to improve him.

He quickly dressed up and left for college. The first thing he did was to ask for an apology from his friend Rohan for his yesterday's misbehavior. His habit of being unsatisfied gradually reduced and vanished – Ashish was now an energetic and a positive guy.

He used to laugh out whenever a depressing thought popped up in his mind. With the positive guidance of his family and friends, he learned how to control his mind and be happy in every situation. He also thanked God for blessing him with many good things in life.

Ashish's takeaway from this episode was that he felt terrible that he had wasted 18 years with his attitude. At the same time, Ashish treated his fight with Rohan as very important, as maybe otherwise, his grandmother wouldn't have shared her life story, and he would have probably lamented all his life!!! Ashish believes it's all our perspective that takes us where we are heading. So, watch yourself… closely.

My take away from Ashish's life is -Try to be happy with what you have in the present and thank the Almighty for his blessings

(As said to me by.......)

LIFE IS PRECIOUS AND BEAUTIFUL

'IT'S TIME TO LIVE AGAIN'

8. Nurture your wise point of view.

An individual point of view

Your experience becomes your knowledge.

Listen to all--gain knowledge--decide things as you want--nurture it--leave scope for flexibility. See that your point of view favors many and is not a sign of rigidity. By spreading goodness, it automatically comes back to you. Become a part of setting a good trend.

Stepping into their shoes

This short story is about a middle-aged school teacher Bhagwati who changed her point of view at a time close to her retirement. She had a set mindset that she felt was the right way to look at things. Her encounter with a young colleague helped Bhagwati evolve to change her perspective and bring out a better version of herself!

It is challenging to change others' points of view, mainly when a seasoned person builds it up over the years. But, knowingly or unknowingly, when exposed to constant and persistent behavior, one can change the thought process … this is what happened with Bhagwati when she met Sunita … and it could happen to you too!

Bhagwati was an experienced, well-respected, sincere, and hardworking high school teacher. She had many awards to her credit and often shared the experiences she had gained over the 24 years of her work life. All the teachers used to get inspired by her ways and adopted them to earn a name. To be known to the school management likewise, Bhagwati left no stone unturned to highlight her work/efforts.

A couple of years before Bhagwati's retirement, a teacher

named Sunita, who hailed from another city, was appointed. She was young, dedicated, focused, hard-working, sincere, energetic, and a passionate teacher by heart and soul. Above all these beautiful qualities, she had one more essential quality-Patience. She was a polite and silent worker and helped anyone who asked. One thing that she stood out from the rest was that she never bragged about her work. She firmly believed her work speaks for her.

It so happened that teachers who took help from her also never spelled out her name or acknowledged Sunita's contribution. As in every organization, some liked Sunita, resented by some, and doubted by some. Just because she never blew her own trumpet.

Bhagwati observed all this and decided to talk to Sunita someday.

It so happened that both of them were free in the same period and were alone in the staff room. Bhagwati went across and sat next to Sunita. The moment Sunita realized, she stood up to greet her out of respect. Bhagwati, out of concern, asked her to sit and listen to her carefully. She said, "I find you to be a perfect human being and an excellent teacher too, but I just wanted to suggest that you blow your own trumpet to be known in your profession. Let others know through you if you do something." She further said, "everyone is taking advantage of you and taking credits themselves. So please be aware of everyone. Everyone is not as good as you are. You may have to repent one day."

Sunita was all ears to Bhagwati and said, "I appreciate and thank you for your concern. Let the others take credit; what has to come to me will surely come; no one can take it away from me; I wish to focus on my work. My work has more power than

                                    Stepping into their shoes

my spoken words." She also said, "I thank God if I am of any help to others as good people surround me. I am also happy that my friends are learning good things from me." Bhagwati tried to convince her, but Sunita was unshakable. She could make out that Bhagwati was saying such things in good faith, but she believed in her point of view.

The teachers around Sunita started knowing her a little more and thought of doing their work by themselves and not disturbing her. It happened in due time, very slowly and gradually. As often said, 'goodness prevails'... slowly working pattern, or the school's atmosphere started changing. There was more silence in the staff room as everyone was busy doing their work rather than asking Sunita to do it. They stopped boasting and started working sincerely.

Everyone became more efficient and productive.

Bhagwati could see the transformation clearly and was extremely glad about the result. The atmosphere at school became more loving and cooperative. The teachers started appreciating others rather than themselves. Since everyone enjoyed each other in the school, the higher authorities also saw the change within the staff. It gradually helped the institution earn a good name and soon became recognized as one of the best in the city.

Bhagwati was ready and open to learning new things as a good teacher. This experience changed her inside out. From now onwards, she knew that work speaks better than words. We need to have a little more patience to see the changes around us.

Again, when Bhagwati and Sunita met in the staff room, Bhagwati said, "Sunita, I have to confess that I never realized what made me the way I am today." She said, " when you joined the school, I saw my replica in you. I used to be very similar to you. I used to be good to all, help everyone and concentrate on my work. I used to get exhausted but still help others. But, I gradually started observing that the others benefitted from my work. I could not see this and gradually became a little selfish. I started speaking about my work, as I thought that was the right thing to be done at that time. Maybe, I did not have the level of patience you have. I polluted my thoughts though it was absolutely against my internal thought process and the real me! I started blowing my own trumpet, and it worked well for me. I developed a belief system that this was only the right way to lead life. I did not even realize when I rigged my point of view. But I am glad you are the same till date."

She said, "Sunita, I was wrong for considering my experiences and point of view as right and yours wrong. You have proven that if everyone focuses on 'work and not words,' the workplace can become more productive and progressive. She thanked Sunita for helping her reset her point of view. Bhagwati appreciated her as a human and blessed her with a perfect future.

This experience altered not only Bhagwati's present but future too. Her belief system changed for the better. She began to understand that being flexible makes our life simpler and happier. She realized that our experiences are not in our hands, but our thoughts are- all we need to do is focus on the task. If something new comes up which is not known to us, we need to be flexible enough to try how to work things out and change our life for the better. Rigidity ultimately leads to messed-up minds and stagnation. We must welcome change with an open heart.

Bhagwati's takeaway was that things and patterns do not always remain the same; then, how can we adopt stuff with the same mindset? We should know where to draw a line and continue being an example to many. Rigidity and stubbornness bring stagnation, and flexibility and going with the flow bring movement and progress. Keep changing for the better in life. Age no bar.

My take away from this story is -Let your good and unique point of view be creative, benefiting many.

(As said to me by Bhagwati)

LIFE IS PRECIOUS AND BEAUTIFUL

'IT'S TIME TO LIVE AGAIN

Stepping into their shoes

9. Follow Your Intuitions

Our inner self always tries to guide us in the right direction, but we tend to ignore it and follow our patent pattern of living life. We love to be in our comfort zone all the time! Come out of it and be happy- Life is all about being happy.

This story is about an entrepreneur called Rohan, a very energetic, progressive, and honest businessman. His story tells us how he suffered substantial financial losses due to his habits and helped himself overcome the failures and lead a better life with proper guidance.

Our stubbornness in considering ourselves right puts us in the well of losses that we repent but cannot come out of. It happens because we refuse to see the wrong in us... the moment we lower our wall of rigidity and stubbornness, we see that light rushing inside. We need to be open-minded to see and adopt that positive change.

Rohan was a very organized, disciplined, and promising entrepreneur. He had established his business across the country and overseas too. And despite the losses he had incurred due to being cheated many times. He trusted people very quickly. He went out of his way to help people but avoided taking help from anyone, even anyone's advice!!!

He somehow didn't see all the aspects of the person he was dealing with and often made incorrect hasty decisions.

Gradually, people around him knew that it was easy to loot him, but no one ever doubted his abilities as he had taken his business to a great height within a short period.

Though he was proud and delighted where he was, he knew he could have been much better placed… he knew something was missing but didn't know what. He thought his ways to be the best.

Rohan shared with me how Arunodaya guided him right and taught him how and where to be cautious, slow down a little in making decisions and become self-reliant and successful.

As usual, Rohan went for a jog early morning. But the morning didn't seem to be as good as the other mornings. Once he was back and ready to leave for the office, he received a call from his CA's office- the person across the line said, "Sir is no more." Rohan was shocked and upset at the sudden young death. His CA not only worked for him but also was a friend and a guide to him. Rohan knew now, that no one was in his CA's office to take care of his business compliances.

Finding a good and learned Chartered Accountant for his company was on Rohan's priority list. His earlier CA office staff suggested CA Mr. Arunodaya. Rohan realized that this person was a pleasant middle-aged personality who was very good at work. He was highly systematic and ensured that his clients didn't lose money. Mr. Arunodaya worked on his father's principles, who was a known and famous Chartered Accountant.

Rohan was boasting about his success stories during their first meeting with him, but Arunodaya could see that Rohan could be fooled easily. Rohan left his office, leaving his company details with Arunodaya.

As soon as Arunodaya went through Rohan's files, he was distraught. He could figure out that Rohan is losing a lot of money due to his hasty decisions. He immediately fixed another meeting with Rohan. He conveyed many things to Rohan but didn't lend any advice or helping hand to reduce the losses Rohan had incurred.

A few days went by, and Arunodaya learned that one of Rohan's customers had defaulted. The amount involved this time was considerable. Rohan was upset and was looking for help.

Arunodaya came to meet Rohan to know what had happened. Rohan broke down in front of Arunodaya. Rohan said, "I am so dedicated and honest, but I do not understand why people do this to me. I have never done anything wrong to anyone; neither have I ever cheated or even thought ill about anyone. I have incurred great losses like this even before but this time it seems difficult to handle the loss. My earlier CA often told me to stay cautious and never trust a person so fast, but I always used to think that if I had not done anything wrong to anyone, why would anyone do wrong to me?! My mind tells me that this person is not reliable, but I ignore that thought and make the same mistake repeatedly. This time the loss is huge, and I need help."

Arunodaya thought this was the right time to help Rohan for lifetime, but he did not give his input; instead, he tried and consoled him. He assured him to provide the right kind of help at the right time. Arunodaya also told Rohan that he would find an excellent solution to this problem. Like always, he trusted his CA. Rohan's gut feeling was that Arunodaya would find a permanent solution to his problems.

After a couple of days, Arunodaya invited Rohan for

lunch. Rohan was quite fond of Arunodaya as he appreciated his commitment and dedication.

After a good lunch, Arunodaya escorted Rohan to his conference room. He showed him a presentation that revealed some facts related to the power of intuition. It showed how our instincts, if paid heed to, can help us and how we can make losses if we ignore our impulses because of probably an unstable mind. Rohan wondered why Arunodaya was telling or teaching him about the power of intuition!!! He should be telling him ways to convert his loss into profit. Rohan doubted whether he was in an office or attending a spiritual discourse. But, he kept quiet and kept listening to him.

Arunodaya told Rohan that he wanted to share his life incident with him to let him understand why this presentation. Rohan was quietly listening to Arunodaya. He said, "when I was preparing for my CA exams, my friends would approach me for my notes, and I would lend them without keeping a copy for myself. My friends would stop answering my phone calls after that." He also told Rohan, "I had to re-work more than often. I even failed an exam due to this habit of mine."

He thoughtfully continued, "As a child, I had always learned that knowledge spreads by sharing. I did the same. But, with the help of my father, I later learned how I could take care of myself and share my knowledge. My father engaged me in concentration and meditation exercises, where I learned to be more stable in my thought process. I have learned to be stable and clear in my decision-making, but also I have learned the real meaning of being a human or having a human life." Smilingly, he added, "it may sound a little weird to you. Still, regular meditation helped me to

   Stepping into their shoes

think categorically. I listen to my intuitions- my intuition is my guiding light."

Arunodaya further showed the total amount Rohan had lost by making hasty decisions and by not following his intuitions. Rohan was listening to him attentively as, Arunodaya was making a lot of sense to him and was surprised to see the exact figures of the excessive losses- Rohan realized his folly.

His inflated self-image worn out, and he found himself closer to reality... somewhere he knew he was close to understanding what was missing in him.

Arunodaya now asked Rohan to relax and meet him the next day. Rohan immediately agreed.

The next day they met. Arunodaya taught some simple exercises and ways to calm Rohan's mind, think categorically, and reach thoughtful decisions. The clarity of thoughts would allow Rohan to hear his intuitions' voice, which will guide Rohan to make sound decisions. Rohan felt so good and promised to continue with this practice.

Soon Rohan was a changed person. He became more cautious in relying upon and took all extra measures not to fall in the same pit ever again! Then one day, Arunodaya called him to discuss the different ways where he could save on his finances and simultaneously be secure about his investments.

Rohan was so grateful to Arunodaya for helping him transform and become a better person. He could now develop more stable and progressive relationships with people. His company showed tremendous improvement within one year, and Rohan gave all credit to Arunodaya. He considered him his mentor and guide, and

Rohan appreciated his dedication and sincerity towards his clients. Rohan found a friend cum mentor in his CA. Arunodaya found a good human in his client and was happy to work with him for his progress.

Rohan's takeaway from this was that the words like concentration, meditation, intuitions, etc., seem outdated. People consider meditation as some activity that takes you away from this world. On the contrary, it helps a person be human and worldly simultaneously. We just have to come out of the pre-conceived notions. We can improve our lives by being a meditator. Goodness attracts goodness. Keep your intentions right and prosper. Help others to grow too. We are the only ones who can help ourselves.

My takeaway from this story is developing and knowing your intuitions' real power. Trust others, being cautious. Avoid falling into the same pit repeatedly, and stop blaming others for your faults.

(As said to me by Rohan)

LIFE IS PRECIOUS AND BEAUTIFUL
'IT'S TIME TO LIVE AGAIN'

Stepping into their shoes

10. Finding your innovative solution

Sometimes leaving it to the child within you

At times, in pursuit of retaining, preserving, and maintaining our image in the public eye, we cannot find solutions to our problems in life.

It's a very heart-warming story of a lady called Disha. She was confined to a so-called socially acceptable or expectable behavior because she could not help herself out of a situation. But, as wisely said, if we are not harming anyone with our behavior, we get help from the Almighty in disguise.

Disha was a knowledgeable public speaker. She was blessed to find a solution to almost any problem and barely believed them to be a problem. She was so spot-on that she already would have an answer before a person could state the problem entirely. She did take pride in doing so but, at the same time, was a very humble and sweet person. She could never think ill of anyone or harm anyone but would always come forward and lend a helping hand whenever and whoever needed. Sometimes even when not required! On the one hand, many benefitted from her instant solutions, and such people looked at her with appreciation. On the other hand, some people criticized her and blamed her for being an impatient listener and a rude instructor…but for her, solving problems came just naturally.

When outside, she had admirers and opposition; she also

faced the same at home. She was married to an amiable and decent person, but unfortunately, he was a little insecure compared to his partner. With her helpful nature, Disha permanently extended her solutions to her husband too, but he was never in the mood to abide by them. Her answering his problems would put him in the defence, and he would either get aggressive or angry and keep doing things his way, falling into more trouble.

The more Disha wanted to help, the more he restrained… Disha internally knew that she had been solving people's problems but could not solve her problem!

She didn't want anyone to know, as her so-called IMAGE as a problem solver would be dim, which she avoided.

Disha kept thinking of a solution as she did not want to lose her husband, whom she loved. According to her, he was a good person with certain flaws which she would rectify as she had solutions for everything. She wore a mask of that knowledge and tried her peculiar solutions. Nothing worked for her, and she was exhausting herself day after day. She kept on struggling silently.

One evening, she reached a point of saturation and could not handle her pain. She decided to ask for help from one of her friends. She trusted Priya would keep the secret to herself and guide her on what to do.

Disha drove to Priya's place. On her way, she was continuously thinking of how to start the conversation...so deep was she in her thoughts that she did not even realize when she reached her destination.

When she rang the doorbell, a lovely middle-aged lady opened the door. It was Priya's mother. She recognized Disha and was

Stepping into their shoes

waiting for her. Priya had to go out for some important work. There was a lot Priya had spoken about Disha to her mother. They greeted each other, and Priya's mother introduced herself as Arunita.

Arunita Ji offered her a cup of tea which Disha accepted immediately and decided to wait for her friend. Both of them sat silently for some time. No later, they started chitchatting and started talking like good friends. It was pretty unusual for both of them, but they enjoyed each other's company. Disha found Arunita Ji to be like-minded and started sharing her experiences with how she solves others' problems immediately. After some time, there was silence, and they started waiting for Priya. Arunita Ji started asking Disha about her personal life to cut the silence. Talking to a motherly figure, Disha initially said all good things about her husband and how she takes care of her personal and professional life. Arunita Ji said, "I am sorry to say but, though you say that you solve everyone's problems instantly, you seem tired or upset for some reason. It seems as if something is constantly bothering you." Only an experienced and kind-hearted person would come to know something like this.

Since Disha was already too disturbed, she immediately started crying uncontrollably. She could not utter even a single word! She had never met a person who would ask about her problem and not for a solution. Disha felt protected and not judged.

Arunita Ji offered her a glass of water to calm down Disha. The lady consoled her by putting her hand on her head and back and asking about her problem. As soon as Disha gathered the will, she started by uttering a few words, then a few sentences, and finally many instances.

Being a kind-hearted person, Arunita Ji heard every word very carefully. Disha narrated one incident after the other, and Arunita Ji kept hearing. Disha told how much she loved her husband and did not want to strain their relations at any cost. She added, saying that he suffers from an inferiority complex, dominates her, fights with her to defend his mistakes, and she is unable to sort things out!!!

There was no one else in the house to interrupt their conversation. Arunita Ji was shaken from within and wanted to help Disha overcome this challenging situation and lead a happy life personally and professionally. But how, she had no idea.

Suddenly, Arunita Ji thought of sharing her own life experience, which was a very innovative idea to handle this situation. The person she was, Arunita Ji, had never shared her personal life with anyone…and Disha – she had met her just some time ago! She started this way. She took Disha's permission to tell her a story. This initially sounded weird and childish to Disha as she discussed something serious about her life. But, due to some unknown reason, Disha said yes.

Arunita Ji politely began the story of a young, energetic girl about to get married. Her friends always loved her for her simple and innocent yet innovative decision-making ability. Everyone would approach her for this and solve their problems. All loved her. Her friends wished her good luck in her married life and also expected her to retain and maintain this lovely ability throughout her life.

As it was an arranged marriage, this young girl hardly knew anything about the new family in her life. As it is true, no two

         Stepping into their shoes

families are the same- so was in her case.

So say, the young girl was happily married, but, at times, her husband would act weird, taunting her for not learning certain things before marriage. According to him, these things were essential to pursue to lead a happy life in a typical family structure. He would sometimes scold her for not serving breakfast on time and for not knowing how to iron clothes. He would scream and fight but give no chance for her to clarify. She loved her husband a lot, but handling this behavior was not under her control.

She could not even share her problem with anyone as everyone seemed normal with this behavior. Often, she would feel deficient, sad, and discouraged. To help herself out, she would drink a glass of water or have a bath to calm herself.

One day, she slept after having a bath after confronting such behavior of her husband. A couple of hours later, she woke up smiling!! During her sleep, she dreamt of her friends. She felt all of them surrounding her, reminding her to light back her abilities- of thinking differently, innovatively, and simply to sort out her problems.

The next day her husband scolded her for not ironing his clothes well; she requested him to teach her as she could not learn ironing before marriage. Her husband said, "I don't have time." She said, "no problem, you can teach me when you are back home or Sunday." By the time it was a Sunday, her husband smilingly confessed that even he did not know how to iron. He realized his mistakes, felt sorry, and was apologetic for his harsh words.

When it came to cooking, she started preparing the food on time. If the dishes weren't tasty, she simply said, "sorry, I will try again." She noticed that her husband did not mean to bother her but spoke so as he had a habit of criticizing. When he saw his wife making reasonable efforts towards whatever he said, he loved her even more.

Gradually, her husband started realizing his mistakes. They began to understand each other well and developed a powerful bond with time. The world never came to know about their internal issues, but on the contrary, over the years, they were a famous couple who shared a lovely bond.

Disha was listening to this with total concentration and analyzing her situation with the words spoken by Arunita Ji. The major suspense was still to be disclosed and came as a surprise to Disha when Arunita Ji said, this young girl was none other than me."

Disha was shocked!!! She had always heard Priya's stories about the strong bonding her parents share.

She jumped out of the sofa, sat near Arunita Ji's feet, and thanked her. She said she could now think of solutions rather than discuss the problems. She could now see that ray of hope to solve her problems.

Arunita Ji further said, " when you start thinking out of the bubble, you find a solution. The solution cannot be seen by the person who believes troubles surround her or thinks she is stuck inside that bubble. Imagine being outside the bubble and finding your new solution.

Never complicate any situation; think about the most straightforward way to deal with it. You can also feel what a child would do in such a situation. You will always find yourself at ease and more confident each time."

Arunita Ji suggested Disha think that the problem she is facing is not her problem but someone else's. "What solution would you give them, as you are good at solving other's problems?"

Soon Priya entered and saw her mother and friend laughing and having fun. They just had a healthy conversation as Disha was feeling light from within. Arunita Ji promised Disha to keep this conversation a secret and that Priya would never know about it for a lifetime. Arunita Ji sighed with relief that she could help a young girl be happy and lead a fulfilling life … by just being a child.

Finally, Disha started acting the same way as told by Arunita Ji. She started finding those simple, innocent solutions to her day-to-day issues and became a happier person. If her husband would leave her towel purposely on the bed to irritate Disha, she would immediately pick it up and say, "let me do something for you; otherwise, you do so much for me, with a sweet smile on her face." If he would purposely not inform Disha about his dinner with friends and expect a fight from Disha's side, she would always say, " I can understand that even you need a break from your routine." At times, she would not even respond to the things on which they used to argue earlier. She stopped being judgemental about her husband's behavior. She also started giving simple solutions to the people, making her more popular as a motivational speaker. She used to thank the Almighty for sending His blessing in disguise.

Disha's husband gradually changed his behavior and started appreciating the positive change in her. He had no clue whatsoever how it all happened…. But they both lived happily ever after.

In Arunita Ji's words, a person gets stuck in their life with problems and tends to blow it out of proportion and remain emotionally scarred. This story could brighten lives and end dark and gloomy chapters of people's lives. We should be willing to be authentic and open-minded and share our experiences with the other generation to pass on a good message which would change the typecast minds of the new and old generations.

My takeaway is that by just starting to think out of our comfort zone or, stay, out of the bubble, we may quickly become problem solvers and add happiness to our lives.

(As said to me by Arunita Ji)

LIFE IS PRECIOUS AND BEAUTIFUL
'IT'S TIME TO LIVE AGAIN'

Stepping into their shoes